Weeks of practice in the simulator pay off as you weave through the asteroid belt, trying to maintain speed the best you can. By the time you're approaching Jupiter, you're twenty-fourth in the race—still good enough to remain in the competition, if you can keep it up.

Your radar tells you that several Protos are coming up fast from behind. These are hot pilots. They probably lost time dodging asteroids, but they're gaining on you now, even though you're traveling more than two hundred miles a second. If they catch up with you, you can kiss your hopes of becoming a Space Hawk good-bye.

You're going to have to cut Jupiter close! But too close could spell your doom!

**THIS IS YOUR CHALLENGE.
YOU HAVE YOUR MISSION. NOW
CHOOSE YOUR FATE.**

**DO YOU HAVE WHAT IT
TAKES TO JOIN THE
MOST ELITE SQUADRON
IN THE GALAXY?**

**Bantam Books in the Choose Your Own Adventure® series
Ask your bookseller for the books you have missed**

A CHOOSE YOUR OWN ADVENTURE® BOOK

SPACE HAWKS™

FASTER THAN LIGHT

Book 1

By Edward Packard

Illustrated by Dave Cockrum

BANTAM BOOKS
NEW YORK • TORONTO • LONDON • SYDNEY • AUCKLAND

RL 5, age 10 and up

FASTER THAN LIGHT
A Bantam Book / August 1991

CHOOSE YOUR OWN ADVENTURE® is a registered
trademark of Bantam Books, a division of
Bantam Doubleday Dell Publishing Group, Inc.
Registered in U.S. Patent and Trademark Office and
elsewhere.

SPACE HAWKS™ is a trademark of Metabooks, Inc.
Original conception of Edward Packard

Cover and interior illustrations by Dave Cockrum
Colors by Judith Fast

ISBN 0-553-28838-5

Published simultaneously in the United States and Canada

Bantam Books are published by Bantam Books, a division of
Bantam Doubleday Dell Publishing Group, Inc. Its trademark,
consisting of the words "Bantam Books" and the portrayal of a
rooster, is Registered in U.S. Patent and Trademark Office and
in other countries. Marca Registrada. Bantam Books, 666 Fifth
Avenue, New York, New York 10103.

PRINTED IN THE UNITED STATES OF AMERICA
OPM   0 9 8 7 6 5 4 3 2 1

FASTER THAN LIGHT

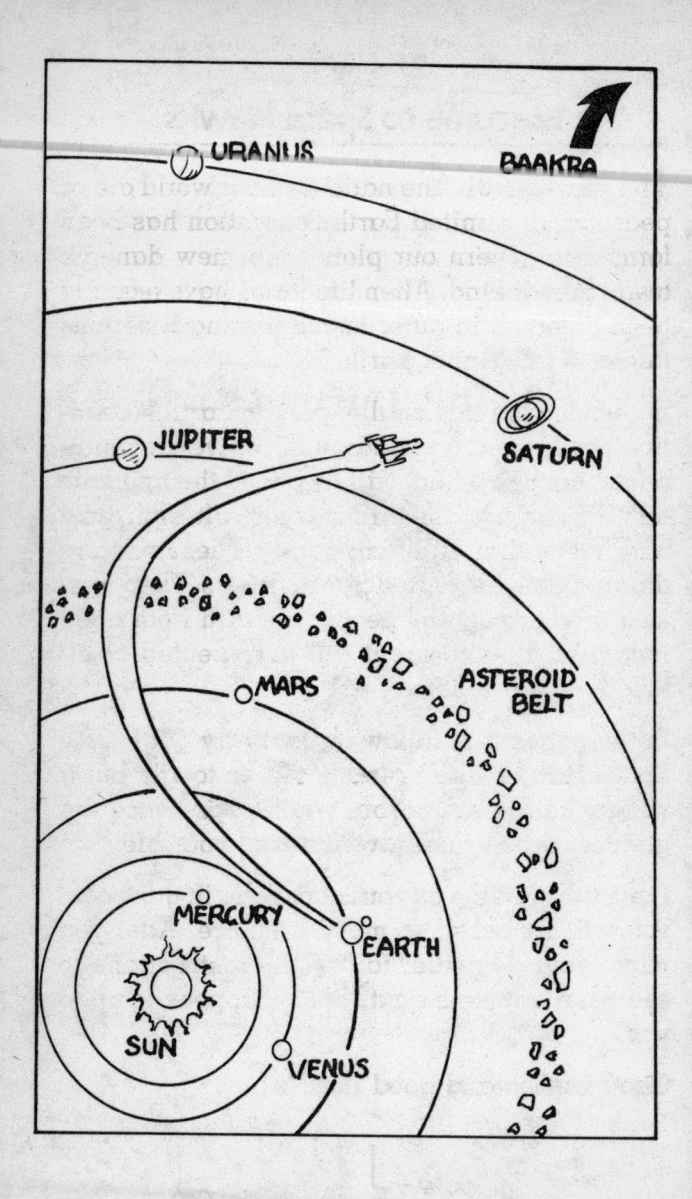

Welcome to Space Hawks

The year is 2101. The nations of our world are at peace, and a united Earth Federation has been formed to govern our planet. But new dangers await humankind. Alien life-forms have recently been detected in outer space, posing a serious threat to the planet Earth.

In response to this challenge, the Earth Federation has formed a squadron of twelve top astronauts, each of whom will fly one of the fantastic new Phantoms, the first spacecraft equipped with faster-than-light capability. These extraordinary pilots are called Space Hawks. Their mission is to protect the people of Earth from alien invasion, and to meet the unexpected challenges of the cosmos.

In the pages that follow, you will try out for the Space Hawks. The training will be tough, but if you make the squadron, you'll experience the greatest thrills and adventures of your life!

From time to time as you read along in this book, you will be asked to make a choice. After you make your decision, follow the instructions to see what happens next. What happens is up to you.

Good wishes and good luck.

Edward Packard

The *Dulcinea*, a sleek, silver-gray spaceship about three stories high and as long as a football field, is resting on the launch deck, its ion-drive humming. A fine, hydrogen vapor mist rises from the twin expulsers.

A gong sounds—the one-minute warning. You give everyone in your family a last hug goodbye, then climb up the ramp and step through the hatchway.

For the past six years, you've been living on Europa, the most beautiful of Jupiter's moons, while your mother and father have been doing geological studies for the Earth Federation. Last month you graduated from the Europa Space Academy, qualifying as a pilot. In fact, you did so well you've been selected for special training in Hawaii.

Though you're barely old enough to apply, you've been invited to try out for the most elite space team in history—the Space Hawks! If you succeed, you'll become one of twelve pilots qualified to fly a new Phantom, the first spacecraft to travel faster than light.

You turn and wave once more. Then the hatch of the great transport slides shut.

You've barely settled into your station when you feel the ship moving as it lifts off from the surface of Europa.

→ → → → → → → → → → → → → → → →

Go on to the next page.

2

Your weight increases until you're pressed deep into the foam padding of your couch. It's a strange sensation—you couldn't get up even if you tried. And yet, if you become a Space Hawk, there will be times in your Phantom when you'll have to endure acceleration much greater than this.

After several minutes the pressure begins to ease. Within half an hour you're almost completely weightless. The *Dulcinea* has stopped accelerating and is now coasting through space at more than a hundred thousand miles an hour.

From the rear viewport you watch Europa shrink to the size of a tiny disc. Then it's lost from view in the glare of the great planet, Jupiter.

You take a walk through the main lounge. The passengers are either reading or working on their notebook computers. You pass the workout room, where several people are doing "weightless" gymnastics. Then you open a door that leads to a small auditorium. The passengers here are sitting in near darkness, gazing out at the brilliant array of stars. They appear to be looking through a thick glass window, but you know it's really a holographic display screen. Beyond it is an eighteen-inch-thick titanium meteorite shield.

Later, when you return to the main lounge, a message is waiting for you—an invitation to visit the captain.

"I'm Knute Jarrson," says the skipper when you arrive on the control deck. "I was delighted to hear we have a Space Hawk candidate on board. If you're selected, you'll get to fly a Phantom. That machine can do rings around this old tub."

"It's hard to believe," you say, glancing at the intricate controls of the great ship. "Still, this must be one of the fastest in the fleet."

The captain beams. "I'm proud of it."

That night you dine with Jarrson and his officers, then turn in early. You've got a big day ahead of you.

When you wake up, the blue-white globe of Earth is hanging in space just outside your viewport. You grab a quick breakfast of honey cakes and nectar, then make your way over to the control deck. Here, several technicians are busy at their consoles.

"We passed the moon," one of them explains. "We're about to enter the Earth's atmosphere."

A warning buzzer sounds, and an android directs you to the deceleration couch. You look through the tiny viewport. Through gaps in the clouds you can see the Hawaiian Islands. They look like a string of green jewels floating on the sea.

→ → → → → → → → → → → → → → → →

Go on to the next page.

4

The *Dulcinea* glides smoothly down toward the island of Hawaii. Ten minutes later it lands on the space force tarmac. As you step onto the boarding ramp, you see the glass-sheathed buildings of the space station in the distance.

A Hovercraft, its small air jets holding it off the ground, is skimming toward you. You recognize the new Space Hawks insignia on its side. As the craft gets closer, you see that Lieutenant Stillwell, the officer who interviewed you when you applied for the program, is driving.

"Jump in!" he calls, as the Hovercraft comes to a stop. "You're the last one to arrive. I don't want you to miss Commander Bradford's welcoming reception."

You climb aboard, and the Hovercraft races over the field at a hundred miles an hour, turns sharply to the right, then glides through the underground passageway leading to Space Hawks Headquarters. Gleaming titanium doors open and close as you pass through. The passageway levels off as Stillwell brings the craft to a stop in front of a sliding door. The two of you get out and enter a niche in the wall. He puts his arm into the circular opening and lets a security scanner read the veins in his wrist, okaying him for clearance. The door slides open.

"Tight security here," you say.

"There has to be," Stillwell says. "Space Hawks technology is far ahead of anything else in the solar system. Pirate spies would stop at nothing to get inside this base."

Stillwell leads you into the auditorium, and you take a seat among the other candidates hoping to become Space Hawks. You cast your eyes over the group. There are young pilots here from almost every country on Earth. You know that every one of them is very smart and athletic; otherwise they wouldn't have been given the chance to try out.

The chatter of voices dies down as Commander Brock Bradford strides to his seat at the head of the table in the front of the room. A huge video screen covers the wall behind him.

Bradford has intense blue eyes and looks as if he's been out in the sun a lot. A native Polynesian, his skin is light brown. He's not a big man, but he's solidly built. You've heard that he was a champion wrestler when he was in school, and you can believe it.

→ → → → → → → → → → → → → → → →

Go on to the next page.

6

The Space Hawks commander looks out over the audience. "Welcome," he finally says. "There are two hundred and forty-seven of you here today—the best young pilots in the solar system. Six weeks from today twelve of you will be chosen to be Space Hawks. The rest of you will probably go home feeling bad. But you needn't. Every one of you is first rate—you had to be to get even this far. Whether you succeed or not in this competition, I wish you good health and good fortune."

The first part of the competition consists mostly of work in classrooms and in space simulators. To be a Space Hawk, you have to learn to be a physicist, a mathematician, and an ambassador, as well as a space pilot. You have to know the solar system inside and out.

At the end of four weeks, most of the other cadets have been dropped from the program. Bradford calls the rest of you in for a meeting.

"There's still almost a hundred of you left," he says. "Congratulations to each of you for making it this far. Tomorrow, the real test begins. For the next exercise I'm assigning each of you one of the new silver-blue, delta-shaped Protos. These are some of the hottest spacecraft in our fleet. They're almost like the Phantoms the Space Hawks will be flying, except they don't have FTL—faster-than-light—capability.

"Now you should know," Bradford says, "the Protos cost twenty billion dollars apiece. Each Phantom, on the other hand, costs eight *hundred* billion. The Earth Federation could only afford to build twelve of them. That's why there will only be twelve Space Hawks selected. Any questions?"

No one speaks up, and Bradford continues. "This exercise is for flying skills only. There will be no simulated combat. I want each of you to take a Proto up one hundred and fifty miles over Hawaii and get in mode 4 line formation. When you're there, wait for my radio command."

Two hours later you're flying in shallow space, high over Hawaii. You're lined up in mode 4— stationary orbit—along with the ninety-three other cadets jockeying for position.

When the last Proto is on station, Bradford radios his order: "You're to race around Jupiter and return to Earth. If you want to become a Space Hawk, you better be one of the first twenty-four to finish. Make use of everything you've learned. Be aggressive, but don't take unnecessary risks. You all have a chance. Now, good luck . . . and begin!"

You apply full power, and your Proto leaps ahead. In a few minutes the whole fleet is hurtling through space.

→ → → → → → → → → → → → → → → →

Go on to the next page.

8

Working feverishly at your computer, you try to set the best course. You can't just head straight for Jupiter though, since the planets are in constant motion. You'll have to head for where Jupiter will be when you get there! You also have to figure out where its moons will be, how much force they will be exerting, and how close you can get to the giant planet without being pulled in by its gravity. Also, since the Earth is racing through space at eighteen miles per second, you need to figure out how best to use Jupiter's gravity to help whip you around on your return trip to Earth, or rather, to where the Earth will be when you get there!

As if that weren't enough, on your way to Jupiter you'll have to weave your way through the asteroid belt, and then out again on your way back. You don't want to slow down, but you don't want to hit one of those asteroids. Some are mountain sized, others no larger than a baseball. Any one of them could be fatal.

Of course you have the finest radar and magnometers ever designed, as well as a great computer to help you—the new XK3-11. But that doesn't mean you won't have to *think*—and you'll have to stay alert every minute. You know it's dangerous, but you're determined to be one of the top twenty-four pilots.

Adrenaline pumping, you push your Proto for all it's worth.

Accelerating through space, you keep your eyes on all three of your display screens at once, giving instructions to the computer every minute. Meanwhile, you keep your hands on the manual controls just in case. If there's an emergency, you'll have to react in microseconds.

Weeks of practice in the simulator pay off as you weave through the asteroid belt, trying to maintain speed the best you can. By the time you're approaching Jupiter, you're twenty-fourth in the race—still good enough to remain in the competition, if you can keep it up.

→ → → → → → → → → → → → → → → →

Go on to the next page.

Your radar tells you that several Protos are coming up fast from behind. These are hot pilots. They probably lost time dodging asteroids, but they're gaining on you now. If they catch up with you, you can kiss your hopes of becoming a Space Hawk good-bye.

You're going to have to cut Jupiter close! You ask the computer for an analysis, and get back the data you need in seconds. The top ten thousand miles of Jupiter's atmosphere are very thin. If you're willing to cut through the thin upper part of the atmosphere, you'll cut out over twenty thousand miles from your trip!

You punch in some figures and switch the computer to voice response. "If I take the short cut, will I be pulled in by Jupiter's gravity?"

The answer comes back.

Not if you maintain your present speed.

There's no time for more questions. You, not the computer, must decide what to do!

→ → → → → → → → → → → → → → → →

If you decide to cut through the upper part of Jupiter's atmosphere, turn to page 15.

If you decide to play it safe and stay above even the thinnest part of the atmosphere, turn to page 28.

"All right," you say. "I'll show you where the Proto is."

"Very good," Manton says. "But don't try to double-cross us." He gestures toward his huge companion. "Dirk, here, wouldn't like it."

Manton leads you to the Rover and tells you to climb in. It's like climbing into a convertible—the whole top of it slides in and out of sight in order to improve visibility while on the ground. And since you're all wearing heated space suits with independent oxygen supplies, you don't need to be in a pressurized environment.

Manton operates the controls, while his over-sized friend sits behind you. You can feel his huge gloved hand resting on your shoulder.

"Just show us where to go," Manton tells you. He doesn't wait for your answer as he jets out of the tunnel.

"That way," you say, pointing. "It's on the other side of the rim."

"Easy enough for the Rover," Manton says with a sickly smile. He accelerates across the crater floor. "We'll take it over the rim. Dirk, put us in the stealth mode. We don't want to be picked up by the other Hawks."

As he's talking, you slip your hand into one of the pockets in your space suit, reaching for your communicator. It's gone. They must have searched you when you were unconscious.

→ → → → → → → → → → → → → → → →

Turn to page 30.

You and your team—Pete, Norie, Alto, and Rapper—set out in your Phantoms on your mission to intercept the Cephids.

Pete has been appointed wing commander. Once you've reached the outer fringes of the solar system, he gives the command to enter the space-time continuum. He plots a re-entry point a few million miles from the leading edge of the Cephid horde. You set your controls and wait for the signal. Your Phantom will then bore a hole into the fabric of space, and emerge trillions of miles away.

When the signal comes, you activate your FTL program. Shimmering light fills your cockpit, and your spacecraft shudders, but nothing else happens.

You instruct the computer to give a status report. Within moments you get an answer.

Space-time block near requested destination. Unable to execute command.

"Are you getting the same thing on your screens as I am?" you ask the other Hawks.

The answer is the same for each of them: "Unable to execute."

→ → → → → → → → → → → → → → → →

Go on to the next page.

14

Pete comes on the open circuit. "Well folks, I guess we have to expect this sort of glitch sometimes. I don't know whether it's a natural event—like an antimatter pocket in the area we want to enter—or whether it's some sort of shield from the Cephids. Either way we just can't seem to get there from here right now. We'll have to follow the other plan. I'll radio back to command. Reset your destination. We're going straight to Baakra."

→ → → → → → → → → → → → → → → →

Turn to page 63.

You've got to take some chances, or you'll never stay ahead of the pilots on your tail. You set your course to enter the thin upper part of the atmosphere, trying to make sure you maintain your present speed and you don't get too low.

You like what you see on your radar. The two Protos closest behind you have climbed farther up, and are falling behind. They don't have what it takes to become a Space Hawk, you think.

Checking the gauges, you realize something's wrong. You have the Proto at full throttle, but you're losing speed. Something's draining your power. What's more, your spacecraft is heating up.

Suddenly you realize what's happening. At the speed you're traveling, even extremely thin air acts as a brake. The added friction is heating the Proto up, slowing *you* down! You pull up the stick. You've got to get out of here!

You check the altimeter. Even though you're trying to climb, it shows that you're still falling. And your forward speed is dropping too.

There's a chance you can make it yet. If you act now, a single blast would send you hurtling straight up, perhaps fast enough to escape Jupiter's gravity. But maybe you should eject.

→ → → → → → → → → → → → → → → →

If you eject, turn to page 103.

*If you try to make it in the Proto,
turn to page 60.*

Turn to page 13.

"I'll go," you say.

Pete looks surprised. "Okay . . . if you're really sure. Norie and I will get our Protos off the ground and be ready to back you up. Keep in touch on band K." He slaps you on the back as you head on out.

When you reach the rim, you peer cautiously into the vast crater below. Before you is a forty-foot drop to a narrow ledge. If you jumped that far on Earth it would mean a broken leg, or worse, but in the light gravity of Tethys, you won't land any harder than if you'd walked off a three-foot-high step back on Earth.

You leap out into space and, using your jet pack to steer, drift gently down to the ledge below. From that point on, the crater wall slopes much more gently, and you have no trouble scrambling down the graveled slope.

Once on the crater floor, you scan the area with your electronic binocs, looking for any sign of the pirates. The sun has now set, and Saturn is high above you. The huge planet and its sweeping rings give out almost as much light as the sun did before it set.

The floor of the crater is a yellow rocky plain, littered with huge boulders, some of them hundreds of feet high. These are fragments of rock that broke apart millions of years ago in some cosmic collision.

→ → → → → → → → → → → → → → → →

Turn to page 19.

"I think Bradford will like the way we performed," you say.

"We'll see, ol' pal," Pete says. "Our commander is tougher than any space pirate."

A short while later, Interplanetary Patrol arrives to pick up the Rover and the pirates. You, Pete, and Norie take off for Earth.

Back at the space command base in Hawaii, you've hardly walked into squadron headquarters when intelligence officers swarm around you, eager to debrief you. Bradford sits in on the meeting. After hearing your report, he comes up and shakes your hand, Pete's, and then Norie's.

"Congratulations, Space Hawks," he says.

It takes you a moment to realize the full meaning of his words. Then, even though you're in heavy Earth gravity, you jump five feet in the air. You made it! You did it! You can hardly believe it—You're a Space Hawk!

→ → → → → → → → → → → → → → → →

Turn to page 36.

You climb to a high point, and scan in all directions, looking especially for radar or laser guns. One large rock looks quite different from the others, and you head toward it. As you get closer you see that its shape is too regular to be natural. Closer still, you realize it's been hollowed out—it's the entrance to a tunnel!

You cautiously start through the tunnel. It curves slowly; after you've gone about fifty yards, you see some light coming from up ahead. You round another curve and stop short. Before you is a cavern, and a spacecraft is parked in the middle of it—the Rover! Its four high wheels are suspended from the sleek gray hull, and a laser cannon protrudes from its bow.

→ → → → → → → → → → → → → → → →

Go on to the next page.

It's obvious how the pirates operate. When they pick up a transport on radar, they fly the Rover out through the tunnel and attack. If they bring the ship down, they cruise out over the terrain and pick up any loot. Then they duck back into the tunnel, where sensors can't detect them.

You stop thinking about this when the butt of a laser pistol comes down on the back of your neck, knocking you out cold.

→ → → → → → → → → → → → → → →

Turn to page 26.

"I don't think it's a good idea for me to go, any more than I think it's a good idea for you to go alone," you tell Pete.

"Well, partner," he says, "I'm on my way."

You and Norie exchange glances. "Good luck," you say. "We'll be airborne, standing by ready to help."

"Thanks, and don't you all worry about me," he says. "Just stay in touch on radio band K. I reckon the pirates can't patch in on that frequency."

You watch Pete step over the rim of the crater and jump.

You rush forward and look over the crest in time to see him landing on a ledge forty feet below. In the light gravity of Tethys, that's like landing on the ground after jumping off a three-foot-high stoop.

The slope beneath the ledge isn't as steep. Pete shouldn't have any trouble getting down to the floor of the crater. Besides, he has a jet pack if he needs a short burst of power to break a fall.

You and Norie hurry back to your Protos. Within minutes you're off the ground, hovering near the outer rim of the crater, waiting for a radio message from Pete.

→ → → → → → → → → → → → → → →

Go on to the next page.

"This is silly," Norie radios. "We could take that Rover out if we just swooped over the rim."

"I agree," you reply, "and Interplanetary Patrol could be halfway here by now if we'd called them in."

"Exactly," Norie answers.

"I hope Pete knows what he's doing."

It's about ten minutes before you hear anything. Then Pete's voice comes through.

"I've activated a proximity jammer, but they spotted me. I'm hiding in a crevice. They've told me to come out or they'll gas me."

"Coordinates?" Norie asks.

"860/313—D 442, if this crazy gyro is working."

"Stall for time," you tell him. "We're on our way."

You signal Norie, and the two of you fly your Protos over the rim, swooping across the yellow rock floor of the crater. You're traveling about five hundred miles an hour, which for a Proto is like being in neutral.

With the coordinates you got from Pete, you're able to superfocus your radar and break through the pirates' stealth shield. In a moment the Rover's image appears on your screen.

"I have it in sight," Norie radios. "Let's go in. Hug the terrain. They may have chem missiles."

"I'm on my way!"

You keep your Proto close to the ground, weaving among the mesas and gigantic boulders

scattered about on the crater floor. Then your eighty-power scope picks up the Rover.

"I have it on visual now," you tell Norie. "Home in your stunner."

She replies, "My visual shows the pirates. They're near the Rover, and they're holding Pete hostage—if we fire, we may knock him out!"

→ → → → → → → → → → → → → → → → →

Go on to the next page.

"We'll have to knock him out then," you say. "He'll be out for a couple of hours, but he'll be okay. We can't avoid it."

Norie's voice is tense. "They have us on radar. They're locking a missile on us—we have six more miles before we're close enough to use our stun guns."

You have a split second to make a decision. The Proto's laser cannon could take out the Rover instantly, but that's out of the question—you'd be taking Pete out too. Yet if you wait until they're in range of your stun ray, a Rover chem missile could finish you off.

Like the quarterback of a football team, you run a list of plays through your head. The Space Hawks have quite a few of them. Brock Bradford call them "ploys." Two of them come to your mind right now. Ploy 16 is a simple one—you and Norie would hug the ground so close that your radar image would be lost behind rocks and ridges. By the time the pirates see you, you'll be right on top of them, firing your stun gun. Trying it over strange terrain could be suicide. But it could work.

Ploy 13—the "sick duck" ploy—might be safer. One of you pretends to make a crash landing. In all likelihood the enemy won't fire because they'll be eager to capture your disabled spacecraft. You or your partner can then surprise them while they're off guard.

The trouble with ploy 13 is that it doesn't always work. It's possible the enemy won't fall for it. It's also possible that you'll fall into a tailspin that you can't get out of and you'll really crash.

Both ploys are risky. But they can work. You haven't much time. You have to make a decision.

→ → → → → → → → → → → → → → → →

If you order ploy 16, turn to page 50.

If you order ploy 13, turn to page 52.

You wake up tied to a mooring post. Two bearded men are looking down at you. You recognize them at once—you've seen their pictures in the "Most Wanted" files. They're the top pirates in the confederacy. If you could capture them, it could lead to a breakup of the worst crime ring in the solar system. The trouble is, you're their prisoner!

The leader, Bull Manton, has the same red beard you've seen in his picture, with a gash across the side where his whiskers won't grow out of the scar tissue underneath. The other guy, Freddy Dirksen, is truly a monster. His face is a sickly white, his eyes look as if they're glazing over, and his mouth is too big for the lower half of his face. He must weigh over three hundred pounds.

"So . . ." Manton says, "thanks for dropping in on us."

You don't say anything. Right now you're just glad you're alive and you can still think straight.

"We know all about you," Manton continues. "You're one of those Space Hawks. Where are your wingmates?"

You don't like hearing this question. It means these guys know more than they should. They must have a very good intelligence operation. Of course, you're not a Space Hawk yet, but if you can outwit these guys you may become one.

"You're not very talkative," Manton says.

"Well, you're going to start talking now. We want to know where your Phantom is parked."

"I don't have a Phantom," you say, "only a Proto. And it's equipped with an antitheft device that you wouldn't want to test."

Manton laughs. He jabs Dirksen standing beside him, who lets out a loud guffaw. "We aren't going to test it," Manton says. "You're going to deactivate it for us."

You can't stand these thugs, but you're also angry at yourself. How did you let yourself get in this mess? And where are Pete and Norie? You've got to think of something fast!

Here's where your rigorous training should pay off. Every Space Hawk candidate has learned over thirty emergency procedures. Brock Bradford calls them "ploys." You have the feeling one of them may come in handy real soon.

As you're thinking about your ploys, Manton unties you, waves a laser pistol in your face, and growls, "Into the Rover. You're going to lead us to your spacecraft."

← ← ← ← ← ← ← ← ← ← ← ← ← ← ← ←

If you show the pirates where your Proto is hidden, turn to page 11.

→ → → → → → → → → → → → → → → →

If you refuse to cooperate, turn to page 34.

You'll never become a Space Hawk if you're pulled in by Jupiter's gravity. You decide to play it safe, keeping yourself clear of even the thinnest layer of the atmosphere. You soon pay a price for this—two other pilots who were behind you suddenly slip by. Now you're chasing *them*!

The asteroid belt lies ahead. A few hours later you're in the midst of it, trying to catch up with the guys who passed you—darting, weaving, diving, sometimes blasting a rock from your path with your laser cannon. It's grueling, and you can't ease up for even a second. But you're getting the feel of your Proto now—you're becoming a hot pilot!

By the time you pass Mars, you've moved up to sixteenth place. After that, no one can catch you. You pass three more Protos on the way home, and a few hours later you cross the finish line over Hawaii, finishing thirteenth—one of the winners!

What a race it was! Two cadets cut Jupiter too close and were pulled into the giant planet. Two others crashed into asteroids. Some cadets fell behind because they plotted faulty courses. Others dropped out because they couldn't take the stress, the speed, and the pressure of it all. Only thirty-two cadets finished the race. The first twenty-four are still in the competition—and you're one of them!

Commander Bradford is waiting on the tarmac

to greet the returning cadets. He shakes your hand when you get out of your Proto.

"Nice going," he says, "but you're all going to have to push yourself even further. Your next test will be in real combat—helping to rid the solar system of a pirate confederacy. If you want to be a Space Hawk, you'll have to round up these pirates and bring them in.

→ → → → → → → → → → → → → → →

Turn to page 107.

A red light flashes on the Rover's instrument panel. Manton hits the brakes.

"That's their search radar," Dirksen yells, picking up Pete and Norie.

"Our stealth shield is holding," Manton says. He stops the Rover. "Train the laser cannon on them. This is our chance!"

Dirksen swings the cannon in narrowing circles as he tries to lock in on one of the Protos. You can't see them because they're in stealth mode, but their secrecy has now been compromised by their active radar. At any moment these two-bit criminals may bring down a twenty-billion-dollar spacecraft, and one of your best friends with it!

You look at the grin on Manton's face. He thinks he's about to make a kill. But he's underestimated what he's up against. You've still got a few tricks up your sleeve, and it's time to use one—ploy 33! With one deft motion, you leap out of the Rover and land neatly on your feet.

When the pirates searched your space suit, they left a few things in your pockets, not knowing they were important. You reach into a pocket and pull out something that looks like an ordinary wad of tissue paper. It contains chemicals that cause it to expand and solidify quickly into something the size and shape of a hand grenade.

You toss this decoy into the Rover and duck. The two pirates jump out and run. Just as you'd

PLOY 33:

hoped, they run long enough for you to get back into the Rover, activate the controls, and drive off!

Flashes of light hit the Rover's hull, but you're not worried—they only have pistols. Seconds later, you're out of range.

→ → → → → → → → → → → → → → →

Go on to the next page.

You switch off the stealth gear and send a coded signal to Norie and Pete on the open channel. There's no reply—they're keeping radio silence—but in less than a minute you see the Protos swooping toward you.

"Hawks 1 and 5," you radio, "I'm in control of the Rover. The pirates are loose—probably hidden. They have jet packs and they're armed with laser pistols."

"Good work, Hawk 3," Pete comes in. "We've spotted them. We have them locked in."

The Protos swoop over the terrain. They're faster than anything in the conventional fleet, but they can also travel slowly, and even hover like a helicopter. You follow them in the Rover.

A flash of light crackles through space. You recognize the yellow and orange colors of a starspear ray—the Proto's stunner.

Then you hear Pete's voice. "We've immobilized the pirates. Setting down—will mark position with a magnesium rocket."

You watch the two Protos land near a cluster of jagged boulders at the far end of a yellowish plain. A marker flare goes up, but you don't need it to find them. It's a flat stretch of about forty miles across the plain to where they set down. The visibility is unlimited, of course, since there's no atmosphere.

You arrive in time to see Pete and Norie frisking the pirates. Norie does a med scan on them.

"They're dazed, but they're okay," she says. "This stun ray really works."

Pete looks over at you. "Did you know we got the two top pirates here?"

"I recognized them," you say. "I've seen their fax pics."

Pete comes up to the Rover and shakes your hand. "You did some great work!"

"Thanks. You and Norie weren't so bad yourselves."

Norie flies you back to your spacecraft, while Pete radios Interplanetary Patrol. "Pirates in custody. Come and get 'em."

← ← ← ← ← ← ← ← ← ← ← ← ← ←

Turn to page 18.

You look Dirksen in the eye. "I don't cooperate with pirates like you," you say.

He glances at his partner, then he turns on you. "You'll cooperate . . . sooner or later." He jabs a laser gun into your ribs. You wince.

These guys will stop at nothing, you realize. You've got to make use of your training. It's time for ploy 14. Your left hand slips along your belt until you feel a tiny button. Your captors don't know it, but your boots are equipped with tiny jets. You press the button, and suddenly you're flying through the air, over the heads of the startled pirates. You land about forty yards away, pick yourself up, and start running toward the Rover. A laser beam lights up the ground near your feet. You feel the heat in one of your heels, but you're almost out of range. In a few seconds you reach the Rover.

The multipurpose craft is one of the newest in the fleet, and you've never been in one before. You're not really sure how it works, and it may have a security lock on it. If you can get it going right away, though, you'll have no problems. If you can't, you'll be trapped inside as the pirates come after you with their laser guns. Maybe you should keep running, and hide among the boulders scattered on the yellow rocky plain.

→ → → → → → → → → → → → → → → →

If you try to start the Rover, turn to page 43.

If you keep running and try to find a hiding place among the boulders, turn to page 47.

PLOY 14:

If you have rubbed out by voice a safe hiding place among the boulders, turn to page 97.

You're not the only one amazed that you made it through the program. A lot of people thought you were too young to succeed. The truth is, you thought so too. But now here you are, about to be inducted into the most elite squadron of pilots in the solar system. You've been given Hawk 3 as your official code name. And in just two weeks you'll be taking off on your first mission—flying one of the new FTL Phantoms, the first spacecraft with faster-than-light capability! Fortunately, you'll have a few days to relax on the beach before you take off on your first mission. After all the training you've been through, you need it!

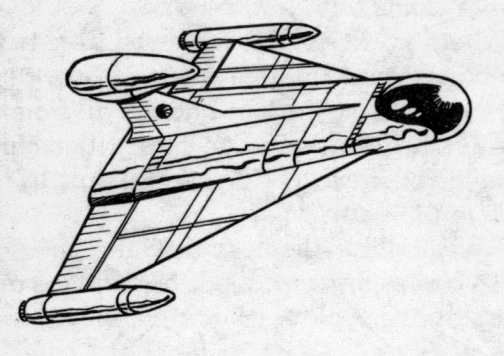

You've just arrived at Waikiki, on Oahu, where you plan to do a little surfing with Pete Walton and Alto Bay, one of the other Hawks. Every Space Hawk is very smart and athletic, but Alto Bay is in a class by himself. A native of Kenya and a member of the Maasai tribe, he has incredibly fast reflexes. You remember back in the academy when he cleared seven feet, eight inches in the high jump.

Stretching out under the tropic sun, you never felt so happy as you do now. Thinking about being a Space Hawk, you close your eyes and listen to the waves rolling up on the shore.

You're just about to fall asleep when your beeper sounds. It's Norie.

"What's up, Norie? I thought you were in Japan climbing Mount Fuji this week."

"I was!" she says. "But I got a call from Commander Bradford. I'm on board the *Mach 5,* headed for Hawaii. He wants us all to report back to the base."

"We just got to the beach! What's up?"

"It's bad. A swarm called the Cephids are approaching the planet Baakra. They need our help fast."

"Wow—we're on our way, Norie." You click off the phone and give a yell.

→ → → → → → → → → → → → → → → →

Go on to the next page.

Alto, riding a big wave, hears you. He gets up on his board, rides it over the crest, and flies through the air like a pole-vaulter coming down after clearing the bar. He lands on his feet in the wash, snakes his board as it flies off the breaker, and starts jogging up the beach. You shake your head in amazement. That guy can do anything.

Pete Walton is a little slower to respond. He's sound asleep, his head buried under a beach towel.

You empty the ice cubes out of the cooler onto his back. That gets him going! He's so mad you're afraid he's going to pick you up and dunk you, but you quickly relay Norie's message. He lets out a low whistle when he hears it. You know what he's thinking. The Cephids were discovered just a few years ago. Not much is known about them, but they are believed to be enormous, insectlike creatures that ride through space on solar winds. They travel in huge congregations, like a plague of locusts, wiping out anything in their path—even whole planets!

→ → → → → → → → → → → → → → → →

Turn to page 40.

You, Pete, and Alto take the next hydrofoil back to the big island of Hawaii, arriving there forty-eight minutes later. You report to the briefing room at Space Hawks Headquarters, where Norie Kiasaka and six other Hawks are already waiting.

Commander Bradford is sitting at the holograph projector in the front of the room. He's working out something on his microcomputer and barely looks up when you walk in.

Bradford is usually all smiles. But right now his mouth is turned down, and there's a dark look in his eyes. After a while he slides the computer back into his shirt pocket.

"Thanks for getting here so fast," he says. "The others are on the way, but they won't arrive till late tonight. I'll fill them in later.

"As you've heard, Federation Command received an emergency transmission from the Baakrans. A vast swarm of Cephids is approaching their planet. The Cephids are still almost a year's travel from their planet, but the Baakrans need help fast. Since Baakra is over six light years away from us here on Earth, conventional spacecraft could never get there in time. It's up to us to do something. If the Cephids overwhelm Baakra, Earth will be their next target."

A murmur of voices fills the briefing room. Bradford holds up a hand for silence. He projects a computer simulation of an area in space, showing where the Cephids are in relation to the Earth and to Baakra.

"I'm dividing you into two teams," he says. "Team A will go directly to Baakra and help them set up their defenses. Team B will intercept the Cephids before they reach Baakra. If team B can't deflect them, it can at least gather information that may help us defend the Baakrans, and the Earth."

Bradford looks around the room. "None of you was selected to be a Space Hawk just because you're a great pilot. Each of you proved something more—that you are smart, resourceful, and that you never give up. Well you're going to need all of those qualities on this mission." He takes out his computer and consults a microscreen. Then he looks straight at you.

"Hawk 3—you, Pete, Alto, and Norie will make a good team. And I want Rapper McCoy to join you. I'm giving your group first choice: I want you to report back in half an hour whether you want the team A mission or the team B mission."

→ → → → → → → → → → → → → →

Go on to the next page.

Bradford adjourns the meeting, and you immediately meet with the other members of your group. Of course you've already worked with Norie and Pete, and you're happy to know you'll be flying with them again. And it will be great to have Alto Bay along. But you've barely met Rapper McCoy before. He's from Brisbane Australia, and used to be a race car driver. There's a scar across his jaw from a road accident. You recall him telling you back in the academy that he signed up for the Space Hawks because he wanted a safer job!

In discussing the pros and cons of each mission, it turns out that the other members of your team are equally divided about which mission they want. Your vote will decide.

→ → → → → → → → → → → → → → → →
If you vote to try and help the Baakrans set up their defenses, turn to page 63.

← ← ← ← ← ← ← ← ← ← ← ← ← ← ← ←
If you vote to try and intercept the Cephids, turn to page 13.

You slide open the Rover's hatch and climb into the pilot's seat. It has one of the most complicated instrument panels you've ever seen. One set of controls is used when the Rover is in the air, and another while it's on the ground. You pull a green "activate" lever and a special screen lights up. A red light flashes over it. These words appear on the screen.

Enter Security Code

Ugh! That's what you were afraid of. You glance out of the viewport. Manton, coming at you, raises his laser pistol. You duck as a blaze of yellow-white light fills the cockpit. When you look up, you see a pool of newly frozen glass on the outer layer of the viewport. The laser melted part of the glass, but it didn't penetrate it.

You look around for a weapon, but there isn't any. You dive into the back compartment and open a storage locker.

The outer hatch opens slowly. You hear Manton's voice. "I know you're hiding back there." In a moment he'll be looking in the back compartment, training his laser pistol on you. You hear him talking to Dirksen. "You didn't leave a laser gun on board, did you?"

"No," Dirksen answers. "I'll just go back there and pluck the little bird from its nest."

→ → → → → → → → → → → → → → → →

Go on to the next page.

When you hear this, you know you've got about three seconds to do something. The locker is filled with all kinds of equipment, and you finally find something you can use—a Mark V magnesium distress flare. You grab it, close your eyes, pull the pin, and hurl it into the forward compartment.

Even with your eyes shut, shielded behind your arm, you can still see the light. At the same time you hear the pirates scream. At this close range they'll be temporarily blinded.

Cautiously, you open your eyes. The cabin is still flooded with light, but the initial burst has passed. While the two men are still groping around, you leap forward and snatch a laser pistol out of Manton's hand. He turns, bellowing, but he still can't see, and you now have him covered.

"Freeze! Hands up, both of you!"

The pirates obey. You order them out of the Rover, keeping your gun on them. They stand on the yellow rocky ground, rubbing their eyes. Their vision is slowly coming back.

→ → → → → → → → → → → → → → → →

Go on to the next page.

You wave the pistol in a tight little circle. "Give me the security code so I can start the Rover."

"Will you let us go?" Dirksen whines.

"You'll get a fair trial," you say. "That's the best I can promise. Give me the code."

Manton is shaking—he's more scared of you than you were of him! He calls out a six-digit number. You enter it into the computer. In a second the Rover's engines rev up.

Suddenly both men are running! By the time you train your laser pistol on them, they're almost out of range. You decide to hold your fire—they can't get far, and it's important to bring them back alive for questioning.

You immediately radio Pete and Norie. Minutes later you see their Protos swooping in. They quickly spot the fleeing pirates, stun them, then land nearby. You radio Interplanetary Patrol, telling them to pick up the pirates and the Rover.

← ← ← ← ← ← ← ← ← ← ← ← ← ←

Turn to page 18.

You run for your life as laser shots from the pirates streak by. You dodge among them, weaving first to the right, then left. Then you see what you want—a crevice between two towering jagged boulders. You duck in. The crevice hooks around, and you're able to get completely out of sight.

You crouch in the rocky niche, wondering where Norie and Pete are, and if the pirates are coming. Sound doesn't travel in a vacuum—there's no chance of hearing them coming.

→ → → → → → → → → → → → → → → →

Go on to the next page.

Cautiously you peer out of your crevice. The Rover is parked only a hundred yards away. But the pirates aren't looking for you, you realize. They have their radar deployed. It's pointed upward, searching for another target—either Pete or Norie!

You reach in your pocket and pull out your radar pulser, which is designed to look like an ordinary pencil. You dart out from your hiding place and run toward the Rover, gambling that the pirates won't see you.

They don't—they're too busy trying to lock their laser gun onto the Protos. When you're fifty yards away, you turn on the pulser and throw it toward the Rover as hard as you can. On Earth, you wouldn't be able to throw something that size and weight more than a few dozen feet. Air resistance would quickly slow it down. But in a vacuum, with gravity as weak as it is here, you could throw the pencil more than a mile if you had to!

The pulser hits the ground a few feet from the Rover. By that time you're back to your hiding place. You dart inside and wait there, hoping Pete or Norie picked up your signal.

You don't have to wait long to find out. A shaft of light descends from the sky, directly striking at the Rover. Manton and Dirksen topple over, hit by a stun ray.

A few minutes later the Protos swoop down,

landing a few dozen yards away. Pete and Norie jump out of their craft, and you run to meet them.

"You okay?" Pete calls to you.

"Great!"

"Glad to hear it. Let's tie up these pirates. Then we'll call Interplanetary Patrol to pick them up and retrieve the Rover."

← ← ← ← ← ← ← ← ← ← ← ← ←

Turn to page 18.

"**P**loy 16," you call over the intercom. At the same time you adjust the thrusters. Your Proto dives, then levels out forty feet above the rocky plain. You ease the throttle until your over-ground speed is down to three hundred knots. Your craft rears and plunges like a bucking bronco as the radar informs the computer of hazards, and the automatic controls respond. One moment you're traveling over the brow of a ridge; next, you're wrenching sharply to the right in order to avoid a gigantic boulder. Norie follows a half mile behind.

If you keep control, turn to page 58.

Ahead of you is a gap in a ridge.

"Stun gun armed," you tell Norie.

A second later you're streaking through the gap. The Rover and the pirates are now in plain view just beyond the valley. You flip the control off auto and bank a few degrees to lock on. A second later you get the tone.

Fire! You look down. It's a hit!

Norie, coming through the gap behind you, screams in your headphones, "Terrain ahead of you."

No time to think—there's a cliff coming at you. Should you lock in the auto pilot and give the computer control in avoiding the cliff; or should you keep control and try to climb straight up by applying power and pulling back the stick?

→ → → → → → → → → → → → → → → →

If you lock in the auto pilot, turn to page 54.

If you keep control, turn to page 58.

PLOY 13:

"**P**loy 13," you radio Norie. "I'll be the sick duck."

You peel off to the right, and Norie to the left. You took on the most dangerous role, and Norie didn't argue. The rule is that whoever proposes a ploy will take the greatest risk.

Two minutes later you approach the canyon. Norie is hovering beyond the opposite rim. You send a radio pulse to her—a signal that you're beginning your run. The moment you fly over the rim, you'll fall into the line of the pirates' laser cannon. You check your ploy 13 computer program. Everything's on line. But you're not going to let yourself be a target for long.

You're crossing the rim—*now!* You instantly put the Proto into an out-of-control spin. Two seconds later you press a button, and a plume of smoke comes out of the tail. You cut over-ground speed to the bottom limit, less than two hundred knots, at the same time wiggling your fins.

It's a very tricky maneuver. You've practiced it only twice. Both times you were flying just above the Earth's moon in a stronger gravitational field. The words of one of Brock Bradford's lectures flashes through your mind:

"There are three great dangers with ploy 13. The first is that you'll do such a good job of looking crippled that you'll actually crash. The second is that you'll be so careful not to crash that the enemy will think you're still a threat to them and, since you're a target, they'll shoot you down. The third danger is that you'll perform the ploy perfectly, but the enemy will still shoot you down anyway."

→ → → → → → → → → → → → → → → →

Turn to page 55.

You lock it back on auto as your Proto swerves past gigantic boulders. You're safely by within seconds, but now, ahead of you, is a sheer cliff rising eight hundred feet in the air. You gasp as you look at it—it's actually sloped toward you!

On autopilot, at the computer-generated signal, the Proto pulls straight up—toward the overhanging rock! There's no time to take over the controls. Perhaps you should eject.

→ → → → → → → → → → → → → → → →

If you stay with it, hoping the Proto will make it, turn to page 106.

If you eject, turn to page 61.

When Bradford said this, there was a lot of laughter in the room. But you're not laughing now—you're scared to death. It's a dangerous game. But there's one thing you've got going for you. The pirates don't want to destroy you— they'd rather have you crash-land. They know you're flying a twenty-billion-dollar machine, and if they could capture it and repair the damage, they could make more than money with it—they could further terrorize the solar system!

It's that hope of theirs—the pirate's lust for power—that saves you. They could have wiped you out with their laser beam, but instead they do nothing, and you pull out of the spin and land less than a mile away, safe behind a cluster of boulders. In a moment the Rover starts toward you. You're not surprised. The pirates are coming to pick up their booty.

Then you spot Norie. Her Proto is swooping over the rim of the crater. The Rover screeches to a halt, kicking up a plume of yellow dust. Its laser cannon swings around toward the new target, but they're too slow for Norie. A spear of light from her Proto strikes them. The Rover's laser cannon swings around aimlessly. The pirates have been stunned out of action!

→ → → → → → → → → → → → → → → →

Go on to the next page.

You turn off your smoke generator, hop out of your Proto, and jet pack over to the scene, arriving just as Norie sets down nearby. Pete's been stunned along with the pirates, but you quickly bring him around. Meanwhile, Norie ties up the pirates.

"Thanks, pal," Pete says. "Let's call Interplanetary Patrol to come in and pick up their Rover—and these pirates along with it."

← ← ← ← ← ← ← ← ← ← ← ← ← ←
Turn to page 18.

You pull back the stick and apply power. You're pressed against your seat at an incredible eleven Gs as the Proto performs a right-angled turn straight up, missing the cluster of gigantic boulders and the cliff that lie in your path. The g-forces are too much for you, however, and you black out.

Your craft continues straight up, while sensors register your brain waves, pulse, and blood pressure. In seconds your mask is flooded with pure oxygen mixed with a stimulant, that prevents you from remaining unconscious and cracking up on one of Saturn's rings. Slowly you begin to come to.

You look groggily at your instruments. The altimeter shows that you're thirteen thousand miles above the surface of Tethys. You quickly take control of the spacecraft and swoop down to the surface, settling down next to Norie, who has already landed near the Rover. The two pirates are still out cold, and Norie has them handcuffed together. She's also revived Pete from your stun ray. He waves at you as you hop out of your craft.

Norie runs toward you, bounding twenty feet at a time. "Nice going," she calls, "that was quite a pull up!"

You motion toward the prisoners. "You did pretty well yourself."

All you can see through Norie's space mask is a big smile.

"Do you realize who they are?" she says. "Dirksen and Manton—they're the top guys in the pirate confederacy!"

"Way to go—we better get Interplanetary Patrol here to cart them off."

"They're on their way," Norie says. "When they get here, let's move out right away. Final selection of the Space Hawks is tomorrow." She elbows your ribs. "We want to be there, right?"

← ← ← ← ← ← ← ← ← ← ← ← ← ←
Turn to page 18.

Trying to make it in the Proto, you keep moving over the planet's surface at about the same rate. Soon you're falling even faster. You pull the stick back and apply maximum power. The Proto's engines roar, but to no avail. You can't even slow the rate of your fall.

In a panic you press the red *eject* button. A half a second later you're catapulted toward the sky. Unfortunately the terrible gravity of Jupiter still has you in its grip. You rise only a few hundred meters before you begin to plummet toward the surface.

In your last few conscious moments, you wonder what it would have been like to be a Space Hawk.

The End

You eject, then feel a dull thud in your head before you pass out. The g-forces are so great you can't stay conscious while you, strapped in your seat, project like a missile above the yellow rocky plains of the tiny moon.

Because of Tethys's very weak gravity, you soar hundreds of miles above the surface before you begin to descend. By then, automatic infusions of oxygen and stimulants bring you to. You're able to use your jet pack to brake your descent, and you set down a half mile from the Rover.

Soon you spot Norie, and jet over to meet her.

"Welcome to Tethys," she says, smiling. "You did a great job stunning the Rover and those pirates."

"Thanks. How are things going here?"

"I woke up Pete—he came around real fast, and he's doing okay. We have the pirates already tied up. And guess what? We've caught the leaders of the pirate confederacy! You, Pete and I are going to be heroes!"

"What about my Proto? Is it okay?"

Norie points toward the horizon. "I'm afraid not, Hawk 3—it's that twisted metal heap over there in the canyon."

→ → → → → → → → → → → → → → →

Go on to the next page.

You shake your head sadly. It was nice of Norie to say you're a hero, but, after cracking up a twenty-billion-dollar Proto, you know you'll never be selected to be a Space Hawk. Maybe you can get a job as a transport pilot. That wouldn't be too bad. Still, it just won't be the same.

The End

MISSION: BAAKRA...

Your team of five Phantoms, headed for Baakra, is soon approaching the outer limits of the solar system.

→ → → → → → → → → → → → → → →
Go on to the next page.

You look back toward the sun. From here it's a tiny, brilliant light in the sky. You can't see the Earth, Mars, Venus, or Mercury. At this distance they would be visible only through a very high powered space telescope. But you can still see Jupiter, Saturn, and Uranus. Through your scope they look like three tiny crescent moons. Neptune and Pluto, the outermost planets, are invisible. They are both about three billion miles away, on the other side of the solar system.

Pete Walton, flying a few hundred miles off your left fin, is leading the group. Beyond him is your surfing pal, Alto Bay. Rapper McCoy and Norie Kiasaka are flying on either side of you.

It should be time now for space-time transit, but something seems to be holding Pete up. In a moment you see what it is, as he keypunches in the news and it appears on your display screen. You groan when you read it. The other Space Hawks team has encountered a space-time disruption and has been ordered to return to the base!

"This is some kettle of fish!" Pete radios.

"It sure is," you reply. "How does this affect our mission?"

"It doesn't. We're going to Baakra," he says. "Set your coordinates, and prepare for space-time transit."

Until now it would take over twenty years for even the fastest Earth Federation ships to reach

Baakra. But with the Phantom you plan to get there within a few weeks! Back in the twentieth century, scientists would have said it would take more than a miracle. Ever since Einstein's theory of relativity was proved to be correct, scientists have agreed that nothing travels faster than light.

Even at top speeds the Phantoms can't get close to it. But now there is a way they can travel faster, not by increasing power, but by piercing the fabric of space-time, creating a wormhole through which they can arrive almost instantly in another part of the universe.

The first attempts at this all failed. Robot ships were blown up, disintegrated, or completely disappeared. It was only when scientists determined that a ship could disappear and leave not a trace of an explosion, not even a single atom behind, that they knew their theory worked—that the ship must have passed into another part of space-time.

→ → → → → → → → → → → → → → → →

Go on to the next page.

It took many more years of research before scientists could find out *where* faster-than-light ships went, and even more years after that before they could begin to control what part of space-time they went to. Only then was the stage set for more efficient and less time consuming interstellar travel.

Even so, the cost of constructing a spacecraft capable of traveling through space-time was, and still is, enormous. That is why, even with the vast resources of the Earth Federation, only twelve such spacecraft have been built, all of them assigned to the Space Hawks. You are proud to be flying one of these fantastic machines, but the responsibility also scares you.

"All right, you Hawks," comes Pete Walton's voice in your headset. "Run through your pretransit checklist, and synchronize your space-time position with the master computer. We'll be there in twenty-six days Earth time; twelve million miles from the planet Baakra. By then, Baakra should be directly between us and its sun."

Seconds later you hear the others reporting.

"Norie in Phantom 5, ready."

"Phantom 2, ready, Pete," says Alto.

"What are you blokes waiting for?" You grin as you hear Rapper's voice. "Hawk 6, A-okay."

You punch a few last factors into your computer. The data you want appears on the screen.

"Phantom 3, ready," you say.

Six minutes pass—the minimum time needed to reprogram safely for faster-than-light transit. Finally a tone sounds, and Pete comes on the air.

"Let's amble on out of here, Hawks. Space suits secure. Countdown . . . three, two, one . . . *Transit!*"

→ → → → → → → → → → → → → → → →

Turn to page 78.

"I don't think we should take part in such a plan," you say. "I think we should talk with the green-furs, and convince them to make peace with the reds."

"Okay," Pete says. "Let's try that—and since it was your idea, Hawk 3, you go for it."

A few hours later, you're flying over Mare Grande, the vast, hollowed-out desert that lies between the lands of the green-furred and the red-furred Baakrans. It's a dried-up ocean that completely separates the two races, and almost circles the globe.

Your radar shows that at one time the ocean was as much as thirty or forty miles deep. The surface is now too hot and too rugged to travel on. There is no way to cross it, except by air, and any aircraft forced down would be trapped. Any survivors would surely die in temperatures hot enough to boil water.

Though it's a ghastly wasteland, this vast, dry ocean supplies enough heat to keep the Baakrans from freezing to death. Their sun—what Earthlings call Barnard's star—is small, dull, and red. Though it appears in the Baakran sky as a large disc—a good deal larger than the sun looks from Earth—it gives off much less heat than the Earth's sun, and looks much the same way the Earth's sun would if you were seeing it through a pall of smoke.

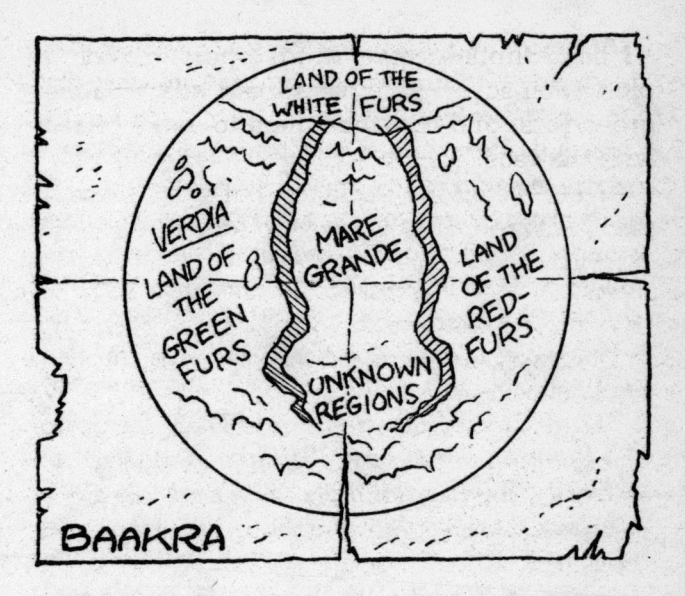

Space Hawks computers have been analyzing the Baakran's language for some time, and they are able to translate what you say into Baakranese. With this program, you're able to broadcast the following message.

"Greetings to all peoples of Baakra. This is Hawk 3, ambassador from the Earth Federation. I am flying over Mare Grande, midway between your two lands. The people of Earth wish to help you settle your civil war, and unite with all of you in defending our planets from the Cephids. Do I have your permission to land?"

→ → → → → → → → → → → → → → → →

Go on to the next page.

After sending this message, you cruise up and down the midline in Mare Grande, hoping that the Buakrans will respond.

For a while you hear nothing. Then a message comes through.

"Approaching spacecraft, this is Z'bong, commander of the Baakran red-furs. We know your message is a trick of the greens. Stay clear or you will be shot down."

Before you can reply, you receive another transmission.

"Earth spacecraft, this is the High Leader of the Baakran green-furs. We have identified you correctly. You may land at our capital, the city of Marle—latitude 33N, bearing 287 from your present location."

You quickly reply. "Thank you, High Leader. I will proceed there at once." Then you send a message to the reds. "Commander Z'bong, this is Hawk 3. We have come from Earth to help you. This is no trick. I expect to get a peace offer from the greens. I hope you will accept it now and help me to mediate a settlement."

There is no response, so you head your Phantom toward the city of Marle, radioing back to Pete Walton and the other Space Hawks with your report.

"Good luck with the green-furs," he radios back. "While you're there, I'll radio Z'bong and try to convince him of our position."

VERDIA...

"Okay, Pete, I hope you have better luck than I did. Over."

The edge of the dry ocean of Mare Grande is formed of jagged cliffs that rise ten or fifteen miles up to the continent's shore. In a few moments they come into view. Verdia, the land beyond the cliffs, looks almost like a scene on Earth, with its green hills, snow-capped mountains, and sparkling lakes.

→ → → → → → → → → → → → → → →

Go on to the next page.

As you get near the coast, you begin to feel worried. Suppose the green-furs imagine you're the enemy. What if they lured you to their coast so they could then shoot you down?

You think of raising your shields, but decide against it. They would be able to see from your radar reflection that you're shielded, and that might make them think your intentions were hostile. Strangely, the safest thing is to come unprotected.

As you drop in altitude you slow your air speed. Within a few moments you're crossing the cliff-line. Banks of laser guns are mounted on the coastal ridges. If they're going to fire, they'll open up any minute.

As you pass over the greens' defenses you hardly dare to breathe. But once safely past the coast, you cruise over the pleasant countryside of Verdia, keeping on the bearing you were told to follow.

In a few minutes you see the skyline of Marle, rising above the soft mists that hang over a long, crescent-shaped lake. Flying over the lake, you can now see the city more clearly. It's a forest of tall, thin towers, from which hang tent-like structures of multicolored lace. Nothing you've ever seen on Earth is remotely like it. You're so fascinated by it all, you almost don't hear the signal that you're receiving, guiding you into the airport. A few minutes later you set the Phantom gracefully down.

As you climb out of your hatch, several five-wheeled electric cars zip down the tarmac to greet you. You slap a translator disc into your hand-held computer and step forward to meet the Baakrans.

From the pictures you've seen on video screens, you were aware that these green-furred aliens look more like baboons than humans. Still, it's a shock to see these apelike creatures walking toward you. What surprises you most is the way they are dressed, wearing elegant crimson cloaks adorned with glittering, golden discs. They appear to be far more intelligent looking than any apes back on Earth!

Though the Baakrans are small—none of them more than four feet high—they look strong and agile. You wouldn't want to get in a Fight with any of them.

The creatures who greet you must have strict orders not to talk. They bow and smile, but say nothing, as they motion you into one of their glass-domed cars. It races down the tarmac, screeching to a halt in front of a cream-colored, arch-shaped building. Between its two sides is a colorful network of wires and ropes, even more intricate than what you saw from the air.

→ → → → → → → → → → → → → → → →

Go on to the next page.

THE BAAKRANS...

The Baakrans show you into a room with about six different levels. Other green-furs are perched on ledges that serve as chairs and tables. One of the Baakrans steps onto the ledge near you. You guess he is the leader.

He looks at you curiously. A series of clicks and whistles comes out of his mouth. It doesn't seem like any human speech, but your handheld translator works perfectly. You hear his words as if he were speaking your language.

"We welcome you, Earthling," he says. "I am Zeldus, High Leader of Verdia. I can see by your strange appearance that you are truly from another planet. We took a chance that you were not a red-fur, and I am glad we did. We hope you can help us settle our war against them, or this planet will have no chance of surviving the Cephid invasion."

"That's why I'm here," you say. "Now what is it that you and the reds are fighting about?"

→ → → → → → → → → → → → → → → →

Go on to the next page.

"Isn't it obvious?" Zeldus replies. "About who will rule the land of the white-furred Baakrans."

"Where is that?" you ask.

"It is the mountainous and frigid region that lies around our north pole—the one place where the lands of the reds and the greens are not separated by the Mare Grande."

"What do the white-furred Baakrans say about this?"

On hearing this question, Zeldus lets out a high-pitched squeal. Your translator is unable to give you its meaning, but you feel quite sure it's a laugh.

"What the white-furs think is not of the slightest importance," Zeldus finally says. "They are a primitive race. They grow no crops, and fish through the ice for a living. They live in houses made of stone, and insulate them with cakes of snow! They have no laser guns or spacecraft, and travel on sleds pulled by arctic deer."

"All the more reason for letting them rule themselves," you say. "They are no threat, either to you or to the red-furs. And for that reason each side can feel safe if you let the white-furs keep their own land."

Zeldus look around at his advisers. There's an exchange of clicks and whistles among them that comes too fast for your translator to decipher.

"No one has ever suggested that," Zeldus says. "It's a strange idea."

"It doesn't matter whether it's a strange idea," you say. "It only matters whether it's a *good* idea."

This brings forth more clicks and whistles. Then Zeldus says, "Maybe you are right, Earthling. Maybe it *is* a good idea. No one on Baakra ever proposed that the white-furs could actually rule themselves and their own land, but perhaps that is necessary, if we are to save our planet."

"If you agree, then we shall propose it to the red-furs," you suggest.

Again, Zeldus confers with his advisers. He then comes over to you and wraps his fingers around your hand. Beneath the fur they feel like steel wires.

"This is what Earthlings do, I am told," Zeldus says, his simian mouth turning up in an almost human smile.

→ → → → → → → → → → → → → → → →

Turn to page 93.

FASTER THAN LIGHT...

You activate the space-time transit program, and a veil of whitish fog passes before your eyes. Your body tingles all over. First you feel hot; then you feel cold. Soon you feel nothing, and then, it seems as if you feel *everything!* Nothing can adequately describe what is happening, but moments later, or is it hours or days?—you can't really tell—a great rush of breath escapes from your lungs, and you feel like yourself again.

You quickly scan your instruments. Everything seems to be okay. The controls are responding properly. Twenty-six Earth days have passed, the computer tells you, just as planned.

The constellations look pretty much as they do from Earth. Even the brightest of them, Orion, looks the same, except the stars in the belt aren't lined up in quite the same way.

The main feature in the sky is a large, dull, reddish-brown disc—the local sun. It fits the computer simulation of Barnard's star precisely. You slap on a filter and train a scope on it. There's a little black disc near the middle of the star. It must be Baakra, just where it's supposed to be—twelve million miles away, directly between you and its sun.

You start a detailed computer systems check. A few seconds later you're on the mike. "This is Hawk 3. Space Hawks, do you read me? Over."

Radar blips are showing up all around you. In a moment you hear the others.

"We read you," says Norie.

"Check," Rapper echoes.

"Hawk 3, it sure took you long enough to get here," says Alto Bay.

"Welcome, Hawk 3," says Pete Walton. "Everything check out okay?"

You glance at the status screen. "A-okay."

→ → → → → → → → → → → → → → → →

Go on to the next page.

"Same all around," Pete says. "Formation code, mode 4. Proceed to Baakra!"

You plug in your instructions and fire the sublight thrusters. The Phantom surges ahead on intercept course with the planet.

Six hours have passed. You're about a million and a half miles out from Baakra. You can now see the planet with your naked eye. It's a greenish-brown crescent, growing larger by the minute.

You're already picking up radio transmissions

from the ground, and the computers have been analyzing them. Each Phantom's computer works on a different portion of data, therefore you have the combined power of all five of them.

By the time you're a million miles from the planet, it looks as big as the moon does from Earth. Pete's voice comes over the radio.

"Space Hawks: The computers have analyzed the transmissions from Baakra. Data will come up on your screens."

You read, *'Situation on planet Baakra: Two races of Baakrans—the red-furs and the green-furs—are engaged in civil war. The greens control the largest continent, but the reds have superior air and space power.'*

"This is awful," you say, "they're fighting each other when they should be preparing to fight the Cephids!"

"They're as crazy as Earthlings used to be when they were fighting with each other," says Alto.

"What are they fighting about?" Norie asks.

"We don't know yet," says Pete.

"We have to stop this!" Norie says.

"You're right, mates," says Rapper. "But how are we going to do that?"

→ → → → → → → → → → → → → → →

Go on to the next page.

"We'll learn how as we go along," Pete says. "They could pick us up on radar any time, so everyone keep on your toes. Commence braking— mode 4-4-7. Norie, try and make contact with the leaders of each side."

"Will do," she answers.

At that moment a small fleet of spacecraft appears on your screen—there must be twenty of them! You're so surprised, it takes you a moment to react.

"Computer identifies them as red-furred fighters," Pete says.

Suddenly you hear Alto. "Combat alert. Bandits firing from 40—5-4-0."

Then the radio goes dead.

The Baakrans are attacking, and your communications are cut off! You were expecting them to welcome you. You didn't have your shields deployed, and you doubt if any of the other Hawks did either! This could mean disaster!

"Keep your shields down, and follow escort to base." This order—translated by your interspecies communication program—flashes on your screen.

"What the—?" Don't they know the Space Hawks came here all the way from Earth to help defend them? The Baakrans must be crazy! Right now you'd just as soon let the Cephids run them over, but you remember your oath as a Space Hawk, and hold off on your judgment.

"Obey orders—this is your final warning!"

You've got to think fast—you can't assume they're bluffing.

You're determined not to surrender. But at sub-light speeds, you doubt if you could defend yourself and dodge this many aliens. And, even though your Phantom can fly faster than light, trying it without proper preparation could be fatal! Still, it may be your only means of escape.

→ → → → → → → → → → → → → → → →

If you attempt an emergency faster-than-light escape, turn to page 97.

If you prepare to defend yourself, turn to page 88.

"Let's join the red-furs," you say.

"Sounds good," Pete replies. "Okay, fix coordinates according to my transponder transmissions. We'll rendezvous with the red fleet and go in on the greens together."

"Roger," you answer, but now you're wondering whether you made the right decision.

Six hours later, the Space Hawks and about twenty red-furred fighters are cruising over Mare Grande, the great hollowed-out area of Baakra. A dried-up ocean, it's now just a desert that separates the planet's two continents. Beyond this vast wasteland lies the rich and fertile land of Verdia—the home of the green-furred Baakrans.

Pete gives the formation code on the common channel. He's patched the red-furred commander, Z'bong, into the code. The Phantoms fan out in a graceful arc, climbing to thirty-five miles above the planet's surface. Speed: four thousand miles an hour.

The twenty red fighters take up stations beneath you.

"Ready for action against the greens," Z'bong reports.

"Very good," Pete says. "You red-furs know when you'll be within range of the greens' lasers. Raise your shields and dive as low as you safely can without risking your ships. While

READY FOR ACTION...

you're drawing their fire, we'll dive straight down with our stun rays. When we have the green defenses out of action, we'll signal you. Then we'll land over by their installations and begin negotiations for unification—you all got that?"

→ → → → → → → → → → → → → → → →

Turn to page 98.

When you regain consciousness, you find yourself still alive, and your Phantom still flying! You break into a smile, thinking about how the Baakran pilots must have felt when your spacecraft vanished from their screens.

But as you scan the heavens around you, you become uneasy. The stars are denser and brighter than you've ever seen them before. And none of the familiar constellations are there.

You request your position from the computer. It flashes as it works on the problem. Helplessly, you wait for the answer. Your fate lies in the millions of microchips in the box in front of you.

Then the answer comes: *No data available.*

What you feared has happened. The emergency leap pierced the fabric of space-time and took you through it to a different part of the galaxy, maybe even to a different galaxy altogether! You could try the transit again, but without knowing where you are, what year it is, or any of the necessary data, there is no way to instruct the computer where to emerge. You might come out in the middle of a star!

Though you're streaking through space at thousands of miles a second, you might as well be going nowhere. You're as marooned as a shipwrecked sailor on a raft, wondering if he'll wash up on a desert island, or simply perish at sea.

The End

The last thing you want to do is battle the Baakrans. After all, the Space Hawks came all this distance to help save them! You're determined to avoid combat if possible. But with red-furred fighters coming straight at you, you know you may have to take them on. Just in case, you prepare to defend yourself.

You raise your shields and peel off sharply, down and to the right, accelerating every second. Light can't curve once it's fired. If you can achieve a high enough percentage of light speed, even a laser beam will miss you.

The lead Baakran fighter alters course, then alters course again. It's on a new intercept with you, and three others that were behind it are coming on at different angles.

"Eyes straight, partner."

When you hear that drawl you almost jump out of your seat—it's Pete Walton! He's broken through the energy shield!

"I read you, Pete—evading left!" you say, swerving and climbing rapidly. Then you lay on reverse thrust.

A laser beam flashes a half mile ahead of you.

"Nicely done," Pete says. "They thought you'd keep accelerating. Oh, oh—above us!"

Your screen shows another Baakran diving from above, and still another converging from the left.

"Three more bandits below us!" Pete yells. "I'll

go after them. You handle the others."

"Thanks." It's still a lot to deal with, you think. But you can't blame Pete—he has his hands full too.

You twist and turn and dive, using every evasion tactic in the book. The Baakrans mimic you. None of them can outmaneuver a Phantom, and yet there are two of them converging on you, and your radar shows two more coming behind them!

So these are Baakran tactics. They have a backup behind each attacker. If the first one gets taken out or evaded, the second one still has a good shot.

They're getting close—there's no room to maneuver. If you fly out of range of one, you'll be flying into range of the other.

→ → → → → → → → → → → → → → → →

Go on to the next page.

Suddenly you're almost blinded by an explosion of light below you. A spacecraft has blown up. You hope it's a Baakran, not Pete or any of the others. But no time to think about it now; you've got your own worries. Only seconds left . . .

Then you remember ploy 30. It's your best shot.

You punch P 30 into the computer. A second later you get the coordinates you need. You pull up your stick, applying left thrust until you enter on a new course and speed. Watching the projected simulation on the screen, you adjust course just as you want. The Baakrans maneuver to keep on you—they're getting closer every second.

When they're almost in range, your computer sounds the tone you've been waiting for. You're right where you want to be, with the oncoming Baakrans lined up on opposite sides of you— they're heading right at you, but also at each other! If the lead one fires, there's a good chance he'll hit his teammate coming from the opposite direction. They may be willing to take this risk, but they're likely to think about it a few seconds first. That should give you the time you need. You drop your shields, and activate emergency escape power. Then you instruct the computer that get-away speed is top priority.

You're flying with your shields down. You could be knocked out with a flashlight beam, as the expression goes. But luckily the Baakrans don't fire. They're altering course, trying to get so they can fire at you without hitting one another.

It's nerve-racking. You almost panic and put your shields up, but the Baakran fighters are now so close, even that wouldn't help you. You can see them steadying on course—they'll lock in on you any second.

Your ready light is on. Without hesitation your finger comes down on the orange button.

→ → → → → → → → → → → → → → → →

Go on to the next page.

You feel yourself blacking out. In your last conscious moment you know that you're accelerating at almost the speed of a laser ray. To the Baakran pilots you're a blur, streaking off of their view screens.

You regain consciousness a few hundred thousand miles away. Automatic braking and course reversal programs are on line. You can relax now.

"Reversal completed," the computer reports. *"On return course to breakout point. ETA, twenty-three minutes."*

So much for relaxing, you think. The ploy 30 program is bringing you back to where you were. You've got to interrupt it and find the other Space Hawks. You know you still may have to face more Baakran fighters. They must be all over the place, like a swarm of angry bees. And this time you could get stung!

→ → → → → → → → → → → → → → → →

Turn to page 95.

Back in space, you receive good news from Pete Walton. While you were talking to the green-furs, he succeeded in convincing the reds that the Space Hawks have not sided with the enemy, but have come to make peace. You tell him of your proposal to the high leader of the greens, and how you also convinced him it was the best way to end the war.

Pete instructs you to join the other Hawks, now cruising near Baakran's moon. "I'll take over from here," he radios. "You take it easy for a while."

While you're on your way to rejoin the others, Pete lands near the capital of the red-furs and presents your proposal to their commander, Z'bong, and Aloo-Tam, the president of their tribe. By the time you reach the other Hawks, he radios back the good news.

"The reds have agreed to a treaty to end the war. Both the reds and the greens will give up their claim to the polar lands. From now on the white-furs will rule themselves!"

The Space Hawks team meets with the leaders of both sides, and the treaty is signed the very next day. The Baakrans also agree to build a fleet of fighters to defend themselves against the Cephids.

→ → → → → → → → → → → → → → → →

Go on to the next page.

The Baakran fighters will array themselves like an umbrella, and try to block the oncoming horde. The Space Hawks will help by rushing in to destroy any Cephids that get through.

It will be several months before the Cephids arrive. In the meantime you and your wingmates must return to Earth and prepare for the eventual showdown. When you come back to Baakra, you will face a new and far more difficult challenge—to save their planet, and Earth also, from the Cephid invaders.

The End

You've covered about one hundred thousand miles in your return when you pick up a spacecraft on your radar. You send out a coded signal, hoping they're Phantoms.

In a moment a low-pitched beep signals a transmission on the secure channel. You turn up the gain, and hear the familiar voice of Alto Bay.

"Hawk 3! You been off on a cruise around the galaxy? We thought we lost you," he says.

"Welcome back, Hawk 3." You smile as you hear Norie's voice.

"What's the status?" you say. "Did Pete make it? He was up against three of them."

The next voice you hear is Pete's. "Why that was nothing, Hawk 3. Just like slappin' at flies."

"We're all okay," Rapper says. "We were able to get through to the Baakran commander of the red-furs, Z'bong, and convince him we were Earthlings and not the enemy. He apologized. His pilots were trigger happy because of the approaching Cephids and because of the war with the green-furs."

You have all four Space Hawks now in view and enlarged on your screen. Their Phantoms look like tiny planets as they reflect the ruddy light of Barnard's star, cruising at idling speed, hardly more than a mile or two per second.

"What now, Pete?" you radio.

→ → → → → → → → → → → → → → → →

Go on to the next page.

"We were just having a little powwow about that," Pete says. "Z'bong and the red-furs say that if we join with them against the green-furs, then the greens will realize it would be hopeless to fight, and they'll surrender. Then the reds can go in and unify the planet. We're divided here on what to do. We're not so sure we should trust Z'bong. Perhaps we should contact the green-furs ourselves. What do you think?"

← ← ← ← ← ← ← ← ← ← ← ← ← ←

If you agree to join with the red-furs,
turn to page 84.

If you advise against it, turn to page 68.

It's risky, but there's only one way to avoid being overrun by these Baakran fighters—you activate Emergency FTL—faster-than-light—mode.

Normal FTL preparation takes six full minutes. Regulations require that Emergency FTL be used only in extreme circumstances, when there is no other apparent means of escape! Well, it sure seems like that now. You activate the procedure and hope it works.

A veil of fog overcomes you. Once again, as you leave space-time you enter that weird state between being and nonbeing.

← ← ← ← ← ← ← ← ← ← ← ← ← ← ←
Turn to page 86.

"Yes, we must destroy them," Z-bong says, "so they will never threaten us again."

"No, you're not listening," Pete says. "We musn't attack. Get that idea out of your furry heads!" He's trying to keep calm, but you can hear the frustration in his voice. "We have to negotiate peace with them, and they must save their laser cannons. You Baakrans will need all the firepower you have for when the Cephids arrive."

"If you say so," Z'bong replies.

But you wonder if he understands.

So far there's been no sign of the green fighters—apparently they're no match for the reds. On the other hand, your lasers are set on stun. The greens don't know that, and their laser defenses may be deadly.

A beeper sounds. There's no turning back. Your status screen starts ticking off the countdown.

Time to vulnerability—2:00 minutes, 1:59, 1:58, 1:57, . . .

"Shields up—drop five hundred meters," you hear Z'bong order his squadron.

Then you hear Pete Walton. "Set stun rays on full—stand by to dive in. Fire stunners at twelve hundred meters and pull up fast. Then circle and set down near the laser arrays—configuration epsilon."

The red Baakrans are now within range of the

green-furs' laser guns. Shafts of white light leap up from the ground. "Stand by to dive!" Pete says.

"Hold it!" Norie shouts.

"Full screen display!" you yell at your computer. Instantly you see the problem. The shields of the red-furs aren't holding. Their spacecraft are going down in flames!

"The greens must have improved their laser cannons," Pete says. "They're penetrating one shield after another!"

"Whoa . . . look," Alto says.

The surviving reds are now diving, their shields down, and their laser guns sending rays of white light blasting toward the ground. Three of the green laser banks explode in a fountain of light, as six more red ships spin out of control. You watch them spiral to the ground.

A great orange ball of smoke and flame rises from a huge explosion below.

You hear Z'bong. "That was their hydrogen depot!" he calls.

→ → → → → → → → → → → → → → → →

Go on to the next page.

THE BATTLE...

"They're wiping each other out!" Alto cries.

"There's no chance for diplomacy now," Pete says. "We'll never bring them together. Take your birds up to sixty-five miles. We'll be out of range there."

You swing your Phantom in a wide arc, accelerating from the deep blue atmosphere into endless, black space. A telescopic image fills you in on the story below—the laser banks of the green-furs have been wiped out, and only two

red-furs are still flying. You watch as they turn back toward their homeland.

"I'm sorry we couldn't help bring peace to their planet," Pete says on the open channel. "We never should have taken Z'bong's word."

"I just hope they realize the mistake they've made, and now try to establish peace," Alto says.

→ → → → → → → → → → → → → → →

Go on to the next page.

"Even so, both the reds and the greens wasted valuable firepower. They could lose to the Cephids now because of this battle," you say.

"And if the Cephids destroy Baakra," Rapper says, "they may destroy the Earth."

"We better get back to the base now and report in," Pete says. "Our leaders must decide on the best strategy. Set course to leave this solar system. We'll pass the outermost planet, then regroup and prepare for time-space transit."

"Wilco," you say into your mike.

A moment later all five Hawks are peeling away from Baakra. In a moment it's just a greenish-brown crescent in the sky.

As you prepare for spacetime transit, you feel happy, but also unsettled. If all goes well, you'll be reaching Earth in a few weeks. Then you'll have time for some surfing and other good fun in Hawaii. But it won't be long before you'll be taking off again in your Phantom. The Cephids are still on their way—sweeping through space like a plague of monstrous locusts. With the Baakrans left almost crippled by their civil war, the task of saving the Earth will take everything the Space Hawks have got.

The End

You grit your teeth and press the red *eject* button. You hear a muffled explosion as you are catapulted out of your Proto. The g-force is tremendous, and you pass out almost immediately.

You're out cold for several minutes before you finally come to. Groggily, you look around. Your space suit has held intact, and you're still rising. You're almost totally helpless now, equipped with only a jet pack and a few days supply of oxygen and food which, luckily, are part of your ejection kit. All your hopes rest on the distress signal that your helmet radio is transmitting. But that signal will never reach the Earth—it's blocked off by the giant planet beneath you.

Jupiter still occupies almost half the sky. You take some bearings with your sextant as a sick feeling comes over you. You've stopped rising, and you're slowly beginning to fall. By now your Proto must have crashed into Jupiter. It seems likely you won't be far behind it.

Suddenly there's a voice in your earphones. "Stand by for rescue!" It's Alto Bay, one of the other cadets! He must have dropped out of the race to look for you!

→ → → → → → → → → → → → → → → →

Go on to the next page.

In a moment you see Alto's Proto, retroblasting to a stop beside you. Seconds later you're through the hatch, and he is applying emergency power to pull away.

"Thanks, buddy," you say, and you've never meant those words more!

"This is some gravity pull," Alto says. "We're barely rising."

You glance at his instrument panel. Suddenly you realize that Alto's craft may have the same fate as yours!

He shakes his head, then points at the computer

screen. "I don't like the looks of the numbers this thing's serving up."

You can't argue—the altitude's barely increasing, yet the rate of fuel expenditure is tremendous. But the Proto has what it takes. Very slowly, it begins to pull away from Jupiter's gravity. In a few hours you're safe and on your way back to Earth.

"Alto," you say, "I'll feel terrible if you're dropped from the competition for not finishing the race."

"I just take life as it comes," he says. "Don't worry."

As it turns out, Alto isn't dropped from the program for rescuing you. In fact, Commander Bradford gives him a special commendation. And surprisingly, you aren't dropped either!

"You showed courage and daring by cutting Jupiter so close," he tells you. "And I blame myself for you losing your Proto. I told everyone not to take any unnecessary risks, but I should have given more of a warning than that. You had reason for believing you were taking a necessary risk to win, and that your Proto could handle it. Therefore, you were only following my instructions. Be at my office tomorrow at 0800."

→ → → → → → → → → → → → → → → →

Turn to page 107.

I can make it, you think. But you're wrong. Two seconds later you smash into the overhanging ledge near the top of the cliff.

At the memorial service held for you a few weeks later, Commander Brock Bradford puts it very well. "We have lost a great flyer and a great cadet. Hawk 3's last act was to help stun the ringleaders of the pirate confederacy and save a fellow Hawk from certain death. Here is an example in valor for all of us."

The End

The next day Commander Bradford assigns everyone to a team. "I'm breaking all of you into eight teams of three pilots each," he says. "Each team will have a separate mission."

You look at your assignment sheet. The two others on your team are Pete Walton and Norie Kiasaka. You got to know them back in the academy. Pete grew up in the mountains of Tennessee. He may talk real slow, but he thinks faster than anyone you've ever met. He's one of the best, all right, even if he does take some awesome risks. It's a wonder he's still alive.

Norie is from Tokyo. She's so small, you might wonder how she got in the program. But you know size has nothing to do with talent. She's one of the best pilots in the world.

At eight the next morning, you, Norie, and Pete assemble in the briefing room. Commander Bradford describes your team's mission.

"You've probably heard that the pirate confederacy has hijacked one of the new L-S Rovers," he begins. "As you know, this is one of the most amazing craft in our fleet. It can travel on land, tunnel underground, remain hidden, and then take off into space."

Pete Walton lets out a low whistle. "That may be a little hard to recapture."

→ → → → → → → → → → → → → → →

Go on to the next page.

Bradford looks at Pete sternly. "I don't care whether it's hard to recapture. I only care that it *is* recaptured. Otherwise, the pirates will use it to prey on passing freighters."

"Do we have any idea where they're keeping it?" Norie asks.

Bradford shakes his head. "We only know that they're operating somewhere within the Saturn system."

"That stands to reason," you say. "They would have lots of hiding places among the rings."

Bradford nods. "And on Saturn's moons. There are plenty of them."

"I can't wait to see the rings up close," Norie says.

"You won't have much time to admire them," Bradford says, scowling. "Your team has the toughest, and most dangerous, assignment of all. Plan to take off at dawn tomorrow. If you locate the Rover and capture any pirates, call Interplanetary Patrol to bring them in; then return here immediately. Now get a good night's sleep—you'll need it. Good luck to all of you!"

At sunrise your team lifts off from Hawaii. Your Proto performs flawlessly, and you feel a tremendous thrill as you streak into the blackness of space.

Bradford has designated Pete to be your team captain. His code name is Hawk 1. Norie's is

Hawk 5, and you are Hawk 3. Pete is flying in the center of the formation. You're in position a few miles off his left fin. Norie is on his right.

"All systems checking out?" Pete radios.

You scan your instruments. "Okay here, Pete."

"A-okay," Norie says.

"Very well—acceleration mode 3.177. I'd like you all to maintain a separation of about seventy-five miles."

"You got it." You ease a crescent-shaped lever down until you get the proper digital readout. Your Proto accelerates, and you're pressed back hard in your seat.

"Take a look at the moon now, or you'll miss it," Norie says. Her Proto is about two hundred miles off your starboard fin, but she sounds as if she's with you in the cockpit.

It's hard *not* to look at the moon. It takes up almost a quarter of the sky. It looks so close you want to reach out and touch it. But it quickly shrinks, then disappears from view, as you race toward Mars and the asteroid belt.

After clearing the asteroid belt, you put your controls on autopilot. It's nighttime back in Hawaii, time to get some shut-eye. Passing a few million miles from Jupiter, you miss the fantastic view because you're now sound asleep.

→ → → → → → → → → → → → → → → →

Go on to the next page.

Later, you, Norie, and Pete assemble in close formation as a fantastic sight fills your starboard viewport—the great planet Saturn with its glittering rings. In the distance you see Titan, Saturn's largest moon, larger even than the planet Mercury. Earth Federation's outermost base is located there.

As you begin to search for the pirates, you practice tactical maneuvers with your teammates. Pete imitates an enemy craft, while you and Norie try to lock in on him.

"Let's see if you buckaroos can catch me," Pete drawls.

You watch him as his Proto accelerates, then darts in among the millions of meteorites in Saturn's third ring.

"Lost him!" Norie exclaims. "He just disappeared from my scope."

"From mine too," you say. "We'll never find him inside the ring. You fly over it; I'll go under. Maybe we'll spot him when he comes out the other side."

A few minutes later you and Norie sight each other on the far side of the ring.

"No sign—wait! I'm getting something now!" Norie says. "It's very dim and shielded—near Tethys—the small moon off our right. It must be him."

"Or the pirates—I've got it too." You switch to the coded channel. "Pete, do you read us?"

No answer.

"Pete, do you read us?"

Still nothing.

"Let's go after the signal," Norie says.

"Roger."

Norie hangs a few miles off your starboard wing as you swoop down past Tethys, putting an electronic scan on the surface.

"Pete couldn't land this fast," Norie says. "Evade!"

A laser beam stabs up from the surface, slicing between your craft and Norie's. You activate jammers, and begin random maneuvers.

Then *swwwwweeeeeeipppp!!!*

Your Proto begins to vibrate. The instruments are going crazy. You can't tell, something might be knocked out.

"Norie, I'm hit, but I'm still flying. I'm peeling off—emergency mode!"

You hear her voice on the open channel. "Pete! Can you read me? Hawk 3 is out of action."

Another laser beam flashes through space. It's meant for Norie, but she's already executed a tight turn and avoids it.

"Rendezvous under ring three," Norie radios.

As you're accelerating on your new course, the computer reports good news—your shields held. The instruments were out for only a few seconds.

→ → → → → → → → → → → → → → → →

Go on to the next page.

Norie pulls alongside your Proto. She's so close you can see her smiling at you through the canopy.

"Well, we found the pirates," you say, "but I'm worried about Pete."

"I'm worried too," she says. "We've got to find out what happened to him."

"Agreed. Did you get a fix on the location of the firing?"

"I cranked it into the computer."

"Okay . . . good, your data is coming up on my screen now. Let's go for it—attack mode 80-20."

"What are you talkin' about, attack mode 80-20?" It's Pete's voice on the open channel! "We need to think this through." His spacecraft comes streaking in alongside you!

"Pete! Where have you been? Someone fired at us!"

"I know," he says. "Luckily I tucked this baby in among the rocks in ring three. My radio blanked out. You two should be more careful though—you looked like a couple of ducks sittin' on a pond.

"We've got to find these pirates and not get shot down trying. Remember what Commander Bradford says—expect the unexpected."

"I expect they're stationed at Tethys," Norie says. "Probably burrowed underground."

"We won't let that stop us," you say. "If we

can't take care of a few two-bit space pirates, we'll never become Space Hawks."

"Right you are, my friend. Let's go in there and get 'em," Pete says. "Maybe we can find the hole where the Rover tunneled under the surface."

"I'll take the lead," you say. "I've got a good approach angle."

Your three Protos peel off, homing in on Tethys. You put yours on low-level-terrain control as you approach the moon's heavily cratered surface, then drop down until you're skimming only a few hundred feet above the ground, winding your way through the valleys between the craters. Pete follows, then Norie.

"They'll do a ground-level radar scan," Norie says.

"Our detectors should give us warning before their scans lock on," you say.

"My guess is that they don't have the technology," Pete says. "If they did, their laser shot would have taken you both out."

"Unless it was just a warning," you say.

"Space pirates don't give warnings," Pete says.

"We're coming up to their surveillance horizon now," Norie says.

→ → → → → → → → → → → → → → →

Go on to the next page.

"Okay," Pete says, "you ready for some fun? I got a bearing on their electronics right now. It's coming from that crater at 045. We'll keep away from it, and set down on this side of the rim."

You land your craft on a ledge a few dozen feet below the crater's rim. Your teammates set down nearby.

Once you're settled on the ground, you take sensor readings. There is no atmosphere. Temperature is minus 173 degrees Celsius—strictly space-suit conditions. You glance upward. Saturn is visible above the horizon. It's enormous—filling almost a quarter of the sky. Its great rings sweep across from one horizon to the other like gigantic rainbows. The sun, which is near the opposite horizon, is very bright, but much smaller than it appears from Earth, and the quality of light is much different than it is on Earth's moon. The reflected light from Saturn's clouds helps soften the landscape, fudging out the shadows.

You check your space suit and bubble helmet, and slip a jet pack over your shoulders. Then you open the hatch and drop to the ground.

Gravity on Tethys is even less than on Earth's moon. In a moment you're hopping around like a kangaroo. It's a strange sensation. You bound toward Pete and Norie, who are coming to meet you. You barely even need your jet pack. You can travel thirty miles an hour just by hopping!

→ → → → → → → → → → → → → → → →

Go on to the next page.

"Let's scale the wall of the crater," Pete suggests over the intercom. "Once we reach the rim, we can scan the inside."

The three of you start to scramble up the slope. You climb fast in the light gravity, but you soon realize it's a long way up, and much steeper than you had judged.

"Let's jet up," Pete says.

A little burst of power from your pack sends you floating up to the rim. Pete and Norie land beside you. From this vantage you peek down at the vast bowl of the crater formed millions, maybe billions, of years before when a huge chunk of rock plummeted down from outer space. The crater floor is more than a thousand feet below.

The three of you unsling your electronic binocs and pan across the floor of the crater.

"I don't see anything unusual. Do you?" Pete asks.

"Not really," Norie says, "but see—there's a faint cloud of dust along the base of the crater."

You zoom in on it. "I wonder . . ."

You unpack a small box with dials on top—an electromagnetic spectrum scanner.

→ → → → → → → → → → → → → → → →

Go on to the next page.

"There's a slight rise in background radioactivity," you say.

"That could be natural. Radiation usually comes from underneath a crater," Norie says.

"It's the only lead we have," Pete says. "We better check it out."

"If our sensors are working, we're now being scanned," you say.

"Okay," Pete says, "that's them. They're probably guarding against aerial attack. I'll go down there on the ground and knock out their radar. You and Norie get your Protos airborne. I'll radio you when it's safe for you to fly over. Then you can neutralize their installation with your stun rays."

You stare at him. "You'd be taking a big chance going down there alone, Pete. We should bring in Interplanetary Patrol with their jammers. Titan's not that far away."

Pete bounds fifteen feet in the air and lands in front of you. "Look, do you all think we'll be chosen as Space Hawks if we have to call for help at the least little problem?"

"We won't be chosen at all if we get ourselves killed first," you say.

"Don't be *macho*, Pete," Norie says, smiling.

"I got selected for Space Hawk training because I *am* macho," Pete says. "Now I don't like giving orders—I like us to agree on things, but I am the team captain, so what I say goes—and

I'm going down there." Then he winks at you.
"Unless you want to go instead."

You gulp. This guy Walton is something.
Maybe it's time to prove that you're more gutsy
than he is!

← ← ← ← ← ← ← ← ← ← ← ← ← ← ←

If you go down into the crater yourself,
turn to page 17.

If you decide to let Pete go instead,
turn to page 21.

ABOUT THE AUTHOR

EDWARD PACKARD is a graduate of Princeton University and Columbia Law School. He developed the unique storytelling approach used in Choose Your Own Adventure books while thinking up stories for his children, Caroline, Andrea, and Wells.

ABOUT THE ILLUSTRATOR

DAVE COCKRUM studied at Southern Illinois University and Colorado State University, then rounded it off with six years in the U.S. Navy. In the early seventies he designed model kits for Aurora, and has worked for over twenty years as a comic-book illustrator at both Marvel and DC Comics, drawing such diverse titles as *Batman*, *The Legion of Super Heroes*, *Star Trek*, and *Ms. Marvel*. He is best known as the cocreator of the new *X-Men*, and for his graphic novel, *The Futurians*. Mr. Cockrum currently lives and works in the Catskill region of New York.